to Sue

Published in 2010 by Windmill Books, LLC
303 Park Avenue South, Suite # 1280, New York, NY 10010-3657

First Published in 2009 by Tiberius Publishing

CREDITS:
Text: Keith Harvey
Illustrator: Paula Hickman

Library of Congress Cataloging-in-Publication Data

Harvey, Keith.
 Tiberius meets Sneaky Cat / written by Keith Harvey ; illustrated by Paula Hickman.
    p. cm. – (Tiberius tales)
 Summary: Tiberius the mouse turns to his friend Drag when Sneaky Cat tries to eat Tiberius for lunch.
 ISBN 978-1-60754-831-7 (library binding) – ISBN 978-1-60754-835-5 (pbk.) – ISBN 978-1-60754-839-3 (6-pack)
 [1. Mice–Fiction. 2. Cats–Fiction. 3. Dragons–Fiction.] I. Hickman, Paula, ill. II. Title.
 PZ7.H26757Ti 2010
 [E]–dc22
                                        2009041109

Manufactured in the United States of America

CPSIA Compliance Information: Batch #BW10W: For futher information contact Windmill Books, New York, New York at 1-866-478-0556.

Tiberius
Meets
Sneaky Cat

Written by **Keith Harvey**

Illustrated by **Paula Hickman**

alphabet
soup™
an imprint of
WINDMILL BOOKS™
New York

Tiberius is a brave, fearless
little mouse with big pink ears . . .

and a very long tail . . .

He is always having lots of exciting adventures.

It was a lovely sunny morning. Tiberius was skipping along when he came to the sign post.

Left

Right

"Should I go left or should I go right?"
he thought.
"I think I'll go right today."

On the way he met several of his friends.
"Good morning, Angus Ladybug," he called.

"You should come out of your shell this
morning, Mr. Snail, it is
far too nice to stay inside,"
he said to old Mr. Snail,
who was getting rather
slow these days.

The flies were up and about early and Tiberius was not too
happy about the way they buzzed around his ears,
but he pretended not to notice.

As he scampered happily along
he thought he saw something
suspicious in the hedges.
He stopped and looked.

He looked again . . .

"I must be seeing things,"
he thought.
"I can't see anything now."

A little farther along he was
sure he heard a noise.
He stopped and listened.

He listened again . . .

"I must be hearing things now," he thought,
but there was not a sound.

He had only walked a few more
steps when suddenly something
shot past him into the hedge.
"I did see something that time.
I must go and investigate!"

9

He poked his head into the hedge, but there was nothing there.
He looked left,   he looked right,

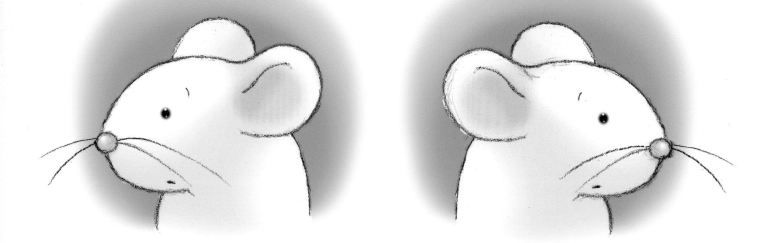

everything was quiet and peaceful. Nothing there at all.

Then he looked
up into a tree . . .

. . . and peeping down
was a **big** black animal
with a white nose
and white paws.

"H-Hello!" said Tiberius
trying to sound friendly.
"Meooow!" said the cat,
"mmm, you look like a nice lunch."
Tiberius looked at him.
The cat started licking his lips.
"Meow, you look like my lunch."

"Your lunch!" said Tiberius in amazement.
"Didn't you know?" said the cat, whose name was Sneaky.
"Cats like to eat mice," and he jumped down from the tree.
"Oh my goodness, don't be silly," said Tiberius as
the cat nearly landed on his tail.

"Oh my goodness!" said Tiberius again as he started to
run away. The cat came bounding after him.

Tiberius dashed in and out of the bushes with Sneaky Cat close behind him.

"Oh dear, what should I do? I don't want to be Sneaky Cat's lunch." The cat kept chasing him and Tiberius kept running.

13

Tiberius then had a brilliant idea.
"I'm going to catch you!" called Sneaky Cat.
"Come on," shouted Tiberius, "see if you can."

Drag's Cave

Tiberius thought it might be fun to teach the cat a lesson.
So he turned and ran and ran toward the hill
where his friend Drag, a dragon, lived.
Sneaky Cat kept following him.

15

Tiberius reached Drag's cave
first and slipped inside.
"Drag, Drag! Where are you?"
he called.

"I'm here, Tiberius. Nice to see you."
"It's nice to see you, Drag, but I need your help," gasped Tiberius,
still out of breath. "I'm being chased by
Sneaky Cat, who thinks I'm his lunch.
I want to teach him a lesson."
He whispered his plan into Drag's ear.

Drag laughed.
"Okay, let's do it" he said and
they both crept outside.
Sneaky Cat was still looking for
Tiberius, calling "Meow –
where are you? I'm going to catch you.
Where are you?"

"I'm here, Sneaky Cat," called Tiberius and waved to him. Sneaky Cat saw him peeping out of the top of a bush.

Sneaky dived into the bush after him. Tiberius disappeared.

"Got you!" he said.

Sneaky Cat thought he had Tiberius by the tail.
But it wasn't Tiberius he had by the tail, it was Drag.

Drag looked down at Sneaky Cat and blew
a huge puff of smoke all over him.
"Oh no!" spluttered Sneaky Cat. "Who are you?"
Drag smiled. "I'm a friend of Tiberius, the little mouse you
have been chasing, and I don't like you chasing him!"
Drag blew another big puff of smoke.

Sneaky Cat looked at Drag, and there was Tiberius sitting on Drag's head smiling at him.

"Like some lunch?" laughed Tiberius.
"Perhaps I'd like some lunch," said Drag,
grabbing at Sneaky Cat's tail.
"Oh no!" said Sneaky.
"I really am very sorry. I won't ever do it again."
"Are you sure?" said Tiberius.
"Y-Yes, yes," said Sneaky Cat.

"Okay," said Tiberius, jumping off Drag's head. "Just one other thing..."
"Anything," said Sneaky Cat.

"I think you had better become a vegetarian and also
we have to be friends," and he held out his hand.
Still trembling Sneaky Cat shook it. "Don't forget—no
more mice pies," said Tiberius.

All three of them smiled at each other.
"We can have lots of adventures together," said Drag.

Sneaky Cat forgot all about eating mice pies for
his lunch because he was so pleased to have made two new friends!